DON'T
MAKE FUN!

by B. Wiseman

Houghton Mifflin Company
Boston   1982

For Pete, Mike and Andy Lee

55 $8.95 American Media Corp. $8.95 7/86

Papa Boar came home from work.
He asked,
"What have we got for dinner?"
Bobby Boar said, "Food."
Papa Boar said, "I'm tired. Don't make fun."

Mama Boar said, "I made stew."
Bobby said, "One and one makes stew."
Papa Boar said, "Please—don't make fun!"

"Ah!" said Papa Boar. "This is good stew."
"No, Papa," said Bobby. "It is BAD stew."

"Look—it made my shirt dirty!"

Mama Boar said, "Eat carefully."
"I can't," said Bobby.
"I have no carefully to eat."

Papa Boar cried, "Bobby!
You spilled your stew!
YOU made your shirt dirty!
Don't make fun!"

After dinner, Papa Boar said, "Bobby—
You make fun at the wrong time.
So, listen—Aunt and Uncle Swine
are coming to visit us tomorrow.
They are coming from far away.
I want them to have a nice visit.
Tomorrow, please—DON'T MAKE FUN!"

Aunt and Uncle Swine
came in a big car.
"Hello! Hello!" Uncle Swine yelled.
"Is THIS your house?
It is so SMALL!
We almost didn't see it!"

Aunt and Uncle Swine
got out of the big car.
Aunt Swine was carrying Baby Swine.

Mama Boar tickled Baby Swine's chin.
Baby Swine stuck out his tongue.

In the house Baby Swine began to cry.
Aunt Swine said,
"He wants to play with your clock."

Uncle Swine lifted Baby Swine
up to the clock.
Baby Swine broke the clock.
Uncle Swine laughed. "Haw! Haw!
Did you see that? Isn't he STRONG?"

Mama Boar asked, "Would you like some tea?"
Uncle Swine yelled, "No! I want coffee!
I like it very strong."
Aunt Swine said, "I want ginger ale.
I like it very cold.
Baby wants cocoa. He likes it very hot."

Papa Boar asked,
"Would anyone like some fruit?
Here are apples and oranges."
Baby Swine threw an apple.
It broke a lamp.
Uncle Swine laughed. "Haw! Haw!
Did you see how far he can throw?"

Bobby Boar gave Baby Swine
toys to play with.
Baby Swine broke the toys.
Uncle Swine laughed. "Haw! Haw!
He can break any toy! Isn't he smart?"

Bobby Boar gave Baby Swine
a coloring book and crayons.
Baby Swine tore the coloring book.

Baby Swine colored the wall.
Uncle Swine laughed. "Haw! Haw!
He likes to color walls! Isn't he cute?"

Mama Boar came in with
coffee, ginger ale, and cocoa.
Uncle Swine yelled,
"This coffee is too weak!
Make me strong coffee!"

Aunt Swine said,
"This ginger ale is too warm.
Put in more ice cubes."

Baby Swine spit cocoa onto the rug.
"Cocoa too cold!" he cried.
"Make cocoa hot!"

Papa Boar asked Uncle Swine,
"How long will you stay with us?"
Uncle Swine said, "A long time!
We like it here a lot."

Then Uncle Swine
slapped Papa Boar on the back.
Papa Boar's glasses fell off.
Uncle Swine laughed. "Haw! Haw! Haw!"

Papa Boar went into the kitchen.

Papa Boar said,
"They want to stay a long time!
Shall I ask them to go?"

"Oh, no," said Mama Boar.
"That would not be polite."
Papa Boar asked, "What shall we DO?"

Bobby Boar said, "I know what to do—
let ME give them the coffee,
the cocoa, and the ginger ale."

Bobby said,
"Here is your coffee, Uncle Swine.
We took out the worm."
"What worm?" asked Uncle Swine.
"The big green worm," said Bobby.
"The one that fell in your coffee."

Bobby told Baby Swine, "Here's your cocoa.
It is very hot. The mouse yelled!"
Baby Swine asked, "What mouse?"
Bobby said, "One of our mice.
The one that put his tail in your cocoa."

"Aunt Swine," said Bobby,
"here is your ginger ale.
I wiped the ice cubes.
They fell on the floor when I took
the big hairy spider
out of your ginger ale."

Bobby got a broom and fly swatter.
He got a baseball bat and hockey stick.
He put on a baseball catcher's mask.
Then he said, "Aunt Swine, Uncle Swine,
you will sleep in the front bedroom.
I will try to chase out the bats—"

"—I will not chase the snakes.
The snakes are nice. They don't bite.
They will just snuggle up in bed
and sleep with you."

Aunt Swine grabbed Baby Swine.

Aunt Swine cried, "I just remembered—"

"—we promised to visit Grandpa Boar.
We can't stay in YOUR house!"
Then Aunt Swine, Uncle Swine,
and Baby Swine got in the big car
and drove away fast.

Papa Boar said, "Bobby, today was
the RIGHT time to make FUN!"
Mama Boar asked, "What would you
like me to make for dinner, Bobby?"

Bobby Boar said, "Food."